Mailbox Quailbox

Mailbox Quailbox

by Margaret Ronay Legum

ILLUSTRATED

BY ROBERT SHETTERLY

ATHENEUM

New York

1985

Library of Congress Cataloging in Publication Data

Legum, Margaret Roberts.
Mailbox, quailbox.

SUMMARY: Mama Quail's newspaper advice column for
animals features some surprising questions and answers.
1. Children's stories, American. [1. Animals—
Fiction.   2. Conduct of life—Fiction.   3. Humorous
stories]   I. Shetterly, Robert, ill.   II. Title.
PZ7.L52155Mai   1985   [Fic]   85-7960
ISBN 0-689-31136-2

Text copyright © 1985 by Margaret Ronay Legum
Illustrations copyright © 1985 by Atheneum Publishers, Inc.
All rights reserved
Published simultaneously in Canada by
Collier Macmillan Canada, Inc.
Text set by Linoprint Composition, New York City
Printed and bound by Maple-Vail, Binghamton, New York
Typography by Mary Ahern
First edition

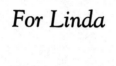

For Linda

Mailbox Quailbox

MAMA QUAIL sat still and waited for the Owl-editor of the *Weekly Territorial* to speak. She, along with many others, had applied for the position of writer for a new feature to be called "Creatures Column."

As it turned out, a Japanese penguin had written to the paper asking advice. The letter had spurred the Owl-editor to create the new column. Furthermore, he decided that all the applicants would have to write a letter of advice to the Japanese penguin. Whoever it was whose advice he took would get the job. All this had happened well over a month ago.

Mama Quail stirred when the Owl-editor finally spoke. "It surprised me, no, *shocked* me, that the Japanese penguin took *your* advice, Mama Quail."

Mama Quail was not surprised, but said nothing. No use to tell the Owl-editor she was known for giving advice.

The editor smiled. "The job is yours. Congratulations!"

Mama Quail sighed with relief. "Good. I'm between broods at the moment. I'd like to start tomorrow." The Owl-editor nodded as Mama Quail went on. "And...I think the first letter in the Creatures Column should be the thank-you letter from the Japanese penguin."

"That's a good idea." The Owl-editor said. Mama Quail nodded, her glorious plume feathering brilliantly in the dusty room.

Dear Mama Quail:

This is a thank-you letter for giving me such good advice. You said a Japanese penguin could sell ice to the Eskimos if he really tried. You were right. I bought a sled complete with dog, painted the sled red and put a bell around Shogun's neck. Now I swoosh around neighborhoods selling slushies and slurpies. Soon as they hear Shogun's bell, the kids come tumbling out of their igloos. Business is good, and I don't even have to pay for ice. It's everywhere. I want to send you a super slushy for sending me the ice shaver. So please pick one of the following flavors.

1. *Sooshie Vanilla with Cherry Blossom Topping (delicate flavor)*
2. *Licorice Soomy Crush with Almond Smash (boys like this one)*
3. *Chocolate Chip Kabooky Cookie with Marshmallow Face (ladies like this)*
4. *Karate Chop on Sunburn Neck (favorite with men)*
5. *Tokyo Tapioca with Ninja Sauce (Sneaks up on you)*
6. *Bon Bon Sigh Blood Orange (my favorite)*
7. *Sam-You-Rye Egg Custard (for the little ones)*

I recommend Bon Bon Sigh Blood Orange (also Shogun's favorite). Mama, you should see these Eskimo kids eat slushies with icicle chopsticks.

Gratefully,
FROSTY FUJI

P.S.   You may keep the pictures.

Dear Mama Quail:

Everyday I play Po-Nuckle with my friend the peacock. In case you don't know, Po-Nuckle is a combination of poker and pinochle. Anyhow, the peacock hates to crush his tail, so before sitting down, he spreads it out and up and around the table, if you know what I mean. My problem is all those eyes. They see every card I have no matter how close I hold them. What can I do? Don't tell me not to play with the peacock. Po-Nuckle is my favorite card game, and he's the only one who knows how to play it.

Close Hold Charlie Crane

Dear Close Hold:

The peacock may not be sitting on his tail, but you must be sitting on your brains. How about playing your cards *under* the table. Think about it.

Mama Quail

Dear Mama Quail:

My little grandmouse lives with me, his grandmother. One time Cheese Whiz stole some jalapena pepper cheese from a Mexican mousetrap. Since then, he absolutely refuses to eat any other kind of cheese. I'm afraid he'll starve. What shall I do? He is driving me up the clock.

Mousetrapped in Minnesota

Dear Mousetrapped:

Move to a Mexican neighborhood.

Mama Quail

Dear Mama Quail:

I'm a momma cat and have two very cute kittens. A gray one and a white one. The gray one is totally selfish and picks on the white one all the time. She slaps her, breaks her toys on purpose, won't let her play or anything. It's terrible. They fight all the time. It's nothing but spitting, scratching and fur flying all day long. The gray one starts it, the white one has to defend herself, and I have talked 'til I'm blue in the face.

Kitty-littered

Dear Kitty-littered

Tell that selfish gray kitten that there are two parts to meow. The ME and the OW. And if she doesn't stop thinking about the ME, you are going to teach her about the OW. She'll find out then that there is a lot more to cry over than spilt milk.

Mama Quail

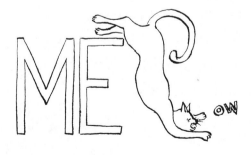

Dear Mama Quail:

My baby duck has yet to quack. All the other ducks his age are quacking like mad. I'm really worried.

Mother Duck

Dear Mother Duck:

Your complaint is quite common. But, there is a very simple cure. Feed him *quack grass.* You can get it at the health food store. Give it to him three times a day before meals. Within a week he will be quacking his head off. He will be quacking so much, you will probably be sorry you ever said anything. If so, please don't write me. There's no way to de-quack a duck.

Mama Quail

Dear Mama Quail:

     Our community is so progressive, we have a ladybug fire chief manning a station of ladybug firefighters. You should see their outfits. Shiny black with red polka dots. They sure draw a lot of attention. And that's the problem. Tourists are coming in droves just to stop by the firehouse so their kids can take pictures. The other day when the alarm sounded, the ladybug fire brigade tried to go to their first fire. But the tourists had the station surrounded, and when the bell rang, everybody went crazy. When they finally got to the fire, everything was burned down. Thank goodness, it was only an empty building. Anyhow, the Town Council called a quick meeting. Half wanted to fire the ladybugs (pardon the pun), but the other half said the tourists brought business to the town. And to make matters worse, the ladybug libbers are waving their hatchets threatening to sue. What shall we do? Please write quick before there's another fire. Everybody's burned up as it is.

                               Firebugged in Omaha

Dear Firebugged in Omaha:

I can understand why the ladybug fire brigade is such a tourist attraction. I'd like to see them myself. Perhaps you should consider having *two* lady bug fire stations. One at each end of town. At least, it'll spread the tourists out and make it easier to get through them. But what you *really* ought to do is have a fire drill every day so that even the tourists learn what they must do. Each station could take turns. Eventually, the novelty of the ladybug firefighters will wear off and things will get back to normal. At least, that's what Floria Flynumb, that famous ladybug libber told me. And she's never wrong.

Mama Quail

P.S.   Please send a picture for my album.

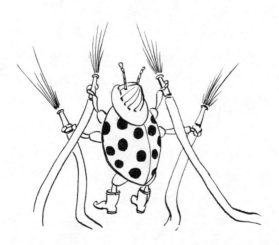

Dear Mama Quail:

I work for a fortune-teller, Madame Gazey. Instead of a crystal ball, she looks into a bubble. My bubble. I'm a goldfish, and I blow the biggest bubbles around. They float out of the bowl and grow bigger in the air. (It's my secret and I'll never tell how it's done.) Anyhow, when the kids manage to grab one without bursting it, Madame Gazey looks into the bubble and reads their fortune. I really enjoy my job because of all the kids that come in here. But, Mama, sometimes I get the blow-drys and can't blow another bubble to save me. Madame Gazey says I better get with it or I'll be out on my finny.

Forever Blowing Bubbles

Dear Forever Blowing Bubbles:

I checked with my goldfish expert, Dr. Gilfinger, and he says you need Bibble Gum. Besides being very nutritious, Bibble Gum is packed with ground-up blowflies. Dr. Gilfinger says just one stick will renew all your blow power. However, he said *never* chew two sticks at once or you'll blow yourself right out of the bowl and land on your finny.

Mama Quail

P.S.   Can you send a picture? Dr. Gilfinger expressed an interest in Madame Gazey.

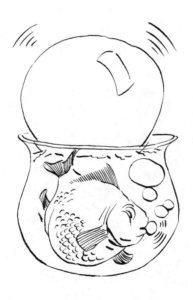

Dear Mama Quail:

We live so far back in the boonies that there isn't even any electricity or gas. And it's very dark in the hutch. My baby bunny is terribly afraid of the dark and desperately needs a night light. Can you come up with any ideas? I have thought and thought and can't think of a thing.

Mama Rabbit

Dear Mama Rabbit

Get a lightning bug. They make wonderful night lights. Give baby bunny a hug for me.

Mama Quail

Dear Mama Quail:

I play the organ every Sunday at my pop's
Hardshelled Baptist Church here in New Orleans.
Afterwards, I meet my friends down on the waterfront.
Us locusts, kaytdids and grasshoppers got a great
dixieland jazz band going. I play lead trumpet. Pop
says it isn't right for the son of a preacher to play in a
dixieland jazz band. How can I get him turned
around? He is so square.

Red Tootie Rah

Dear Red Tootie Rah:

Change you practice place. Stand right smack in front of the church and play "When The Saints Go Marching In." Play it a lot. It'll pack the pews. When your pop, the preacher, sees standing room only, he'll come around. He's probably forgotten about those famous trumpeters in the Bible. Joshua and Gabriel! You might remind him. Keep tootin'!

Mama Quail

Dear Mama Quail:

My youngest snapping turtle, Whippersnap, is in the first grade and having behavior problems. Teacher is always sending home notes. Whippersnap doesn't want to do anything but snap. At the boy next to him. At the girl in front of him. And at the teacher every time she gets near. Even the school psychologist acts scared of him. He's no help at all. The teacher and I have just about given up. Help! I hate to say it, but please make it snappy.

Whippersnap's Mom

Dear Whippersnap's Mom:

There is no reason for Whippersnapper to behave in such a manner, even if he is a snapping turtle. I have a solution. Feed him a bowl of snapdragons every morning before school. Snapdragons give snapping turtles hiccups. Whippersnap will be so busy hiccuping he won't have time to snap. Try it for one week. After that, he'll be so relieved not to hiccup, he'll be glad to sit quietly in class. Let me know how it works out. I care.

Mama Quail

P.S.   I talked with our local expert psychologist, Pop Shrink, and he said since snapping comes natural to snapping turtles, don't be alarmed if the snapdragon cure doesn't work. If it doesn't let me know. Pop Shrink comes up with some crazy cures, but they always seem to work.   MQ

Dear Mama Quail:

You won't believe what's happening here. The old rooster that crowed cock-a-doodle do every morning up and died. And guess what? The farmer says me and the other roosters have to audition for the job. He says the good old days of just crowing cock-a-doodle do are gone forever. Then he gave us a list of what he wants us to crow for the audition. Mama, you will not believe the list. Read on.

Bock-a-zoodle coo
Cock-a-yoodle doo
Dock-a-xoodle foo
Fock-a-woodle goo
Gock-a-voodle hoo
Hock-a-toodle joo
Jock-a-soodle koo
Kock-a-roodle loo
Lock-a-poodle moo
Mock-a-noodle noo
Nock-a-moodle poo
Pock-a-loodle roo
Rock-a-koodle soo
Sock-a-joodle too
Tock-a-hoodle voo
Vock-a-goodle woo
Wock-a-foodle xoo
Xock-a-doodle yoo
Yock-a-coodle zoo
Zock-a-boodle boo

And if you think reading *them is hard, try* crowing *them.*

The Phantom Bantom

Dear Phantom Bantom:

WHEW! You're absolutely right. I had my kids say the list out loud and no one got past Vock-a-goodle woo. As for Lock-a-poodle moo... is he kidding? I guess you roosters will just have to "crow" with the times. Sorry about that. However, far as I'm concerned, nothing will ever replace that good old-fashioned sound of cock-a-doodle do. Some things should never be changed.

Mama Quail

Wock-a-foodle-xoo

Dear Mama Quail:

Since the Cabbage Patch and Lettuce Head Dolls have proved so popular, I have come up with my own creation. It could be the next craze. I stuff all kinds of dried fruit into old, grungy nylons. Then squeeze and push them into doll shapes and tuck stringy bows everywhere. They are really cute. The ones with the prune eyes are cutest. I call them "Ugli Fruit Dolls." Do you think I have a chance?

Anty Maim

Dear Anty Maim:

Send a picture. Then I'll tell you.

Mama Quail

Dear Mama Quail:

When my son, the lion, left the jungle for the big city to make his fortune, I was happy. I figured he'd be a lionbacker for the Sittsburg Peelers. Mama, you can imagine how shocked I was when he came back. Would you believe that his beautiful, luxurious mane has been braided, plaited and corn-rowed into a Bo Derek hairdo. He's even changed his name. To Beau. Get it? Talk about a blow to our pride. As for the other lions, they are roaring jealous of the attention Beau's getting from their mates. And when the hunters come, they ignore the other lions to take Beau's picture. As for Beau, he just lays around all day. He refuses to work, and we need the money.

Heartsick in Kenya

Dear Heartsick in Kenya:

Why not go into business right there? Beau wouldn't even have to leave home to make his fortune. Start by charging the hunters for taking his picture. But a real fortune would be made if Beau could model for a high-fashion hairdresser. There is such a shop in Kenya. It's called "The Mane Man." Let me know how Beau makes out. I'm really curious.

Mama Quail

Dear Mama Quail:

I'm very happy with the humans who take care of us except for one thing. My husband, Cheep Shotz, the parakeet, is the life of their parties. They pour root beer into a glass like a bird bath, then open the cage. Cheep Shotz can't wait to dive in. He's wild about root beer baths. Says the froth reminds him of the ocean. He flips, flaps and flops and sips. And sips. The humans can't stop laughing at his antics. Then they stick him back into the cage for Act Two. Cheep Shotz never disappoints them. He goes right into his Tarzan bit on the swings. I sure would like to get my beak into the human who taught him that yell. There's more. Cheep Shotz gets sick from all that swinging and throws up. Guess who has to clean it up. Please write before Friday. That's the next party.

Wife of the Life of the Party

Dear Wife of:

I'm sending this by Express Mail. Hope you get it in time. My birdman Ferd Birdwiser, said to put half a teaspoon of green poppyseed into Cheep Shotz's food just before party time. It will keep him from getting sick and you won't have that mess. I say go one step further and take all the swings down. No way can he do his Tarzan thing without those swings. Believe me, it'll work. I've been there.

Mama Quail

Dear Mama Quail:

My youngest octopus is in the first grade and having the worst time. None of this classmates will play with him. Especially, baseball, football or basketball. Because, when little octopus catches the ball, he wraps his tentacles around and won't let go. To get their ball back, his classmates have to tug and pull with all their might. This makes little octopus's suction cups very sore. He comes home crying every day and says everybody calls him "All-Day Sucker." What can I do?

All-Day Sucker's Mom

Dear All-Day Sucker's Mom:

Rub some Vaseline into each of his suction cups. He'll lose his grip on all the balls, but he'll gain lots of playmates. He'll come home happy, and you won't have to grease his cups anymore. Lots of luck.

Mama Quail

Dear Mama Quail:

       I'm writing for help. You've heard of watchdogs? Well, I'm a watchgoose. I live in the yard and watch my owner's house, night and day. If a stranger appears, I honk and honk. Nobody gets by me So everything is fine, except that I wish I had a pond. The kid next door has one, and he isn't even a goose. Not only that, he can't even swim. His mama keeps sticking him in the water and then going inside. The dumb kid is forever falling over, and he can't get up. I spend half my time honking to get her attention. Then she comes and rescues the kid. How can I tell my owners I'd like to have a pond, too. I think I deserve it.

Honky

Dear Honky:

I checked with my expert on these matters, Mother Goose's granddaughter, Person Goose. She said, after the mother puts the baby in the pond, fly over the fence and wade right in. You can paddle around the baby and keep him from falling over. When the mother sees how you are helping out, she will let you babysit for the privilege of using the pond. There's more than one way to cook a goose. Oh, sorry about that.

Mama Quail

Dear Mama Quail:

I fly with the famous Blue Angelfish Squadron. We do all those tricks that the Blue Angels do. Anyhow, we've got a problem. Every time we skim a few feet above the ocean, just before we break into the fleur-de-lis, there's this whale there, waiting for us. Soon as we pass over him, he throws up a spout of water you wouldn't believe. It completely wrecks our act and we all fall into the ocean. What can we do? No matter where we do our stunts, he's there, waiting for us.

Blue Angelfish One

Dear Blue Angelfish One

  I suspect that the poor whale wishes he could fly, and only wants to get into the act. So why not let him. Pretend his spout is a fountain of water. When you dive through it, drop some instant rainbow pellets, and you will have a spectacular water show for a grand finale. Try it. You'll like it.

Mama Quail

Dear Mama Quail:

Every year the sea creatures in my classroom decorate the Sea World Christmas Tree. Besides seashells, of course, the tree is decorated with sea horses, sea urchins, sea anemones, and sea fans. Everything was fine until we put the starfish on top. He got scared of the height, couldn't hang on and fell off, breaking one of his points. When I told him he could no longer be the Christmas Starfish, he cried. One of his points is in a cast. It would look awful. He's still crying. I'm going nuts from his crying. HELP and please write before Christmas.

Sea Creatures Teacher

Dear Sea Creatures Teacher:

Since he's so determined, it seems a shame not to let the starfish help himself. Glue some glitter on his cast and tie him up there with a shiny ribbon. Tell him not to look down. I've never heard of a Sea World Christmas Tree. Sounds darling. You didn't mention sea holly. Great to drape on branches. Let me know how the starfish makes out. Merry Christmas.

Mama Quail

Dear Mama Quail:

My butterfly, Tassie, is hyperactive. She never sits still for a second. She flits around and flutters around so much, it makes me dizzy all over. And I don't have the time or energy to run after her all day long. She really wears me out. Do you have any suggestions?

Butterfly'd Out

Dear Butterfly'd Out:

Hang in there. I have good news. Put Tassie on buttercup pollen right away. Also, butterwort, butterbur and butterweed pollen. In fact, any herb or flower with the word "butter" in it will do wonders in calming her down. Let me know how things work out. I love butterflies.

Mama Quail

Dear Mama Quail:

My little elephant, Fipple, sucks his trunk. ALL THE TIME! I have done everything possible to break him of this habit. One time, I even tied his trunk up between his ears, but the rope broke. I'm getting desperate. Please help.

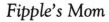
Fipple's Mom

Dear Fipple's Mom:

The best thing to do is take Fipple over to the community firehouse and ask the firemen to take him for a ride. He'll be so busy waving to friends with his trunk, he'll forget about sucking it. Best of all, when there really is a fire, Fipple can help. While the firemen are putting out the big fires, Fipple could be spraying water on the very small fires. Keeping him busy will help overcome his habit. Who knows? The firemen might adopt him as their mascot. Do let me know how little Fipple makes out. I care.

Mama Quail

Dear Mama Quail:

Mockie, my little tortoise, is super shy. He just wants to hide in his shell all day long. The teacher says he's afraid to stick his neck out. His classmates call him names. Like "Mockie Shell Shockie." Can you help?

Mockie's Mom

Dear Mockie's Mom:

Find a thousand-legger who's wild about tap dancing. Put him on Mockie's shell. The tap dancing will make Mockie wonder what's happening. When he sticks his head out to see, have a plate of fruit flies ready for him to eat. Do this every day, until he sticks his neck out on his own. You'll know he's cured when he eats the thousand-legger.

Mama Quail

Dear Mama Quail:

     I am retired and live in a pond in the middle of a golf course in Florida. I have a nice job that keeps me going. I get a dime for finding every ball that drops into the pond. Not bad for an old 'gater. Right? However, I am having a problem with my grandson, who is spending the summer with me. Algie spends all his time running around the golf course gobbling up every ball he sees. When he gets a mouthful, he races back to the pond and tosses them in. He says he's helping his grandgater make more money. Mama Quail, I've done everything to make him stop, but he won't listen. And you know how golfers get when they can't find their balls. If they ever catch Algie stealing them, I'm afraid to think what will happen. Please tell me what to do. I'm stuck with him for the summer.

Retired but **INDEPONDENT**

Dear INDEPONDENT (you old cutie):

I've heard of gater-aid, but this is ridiculous. Now then, I checked with our local golf pro, and he came up with a grand idea. Golfers seldom find their balls when they are hit into high grass. In fact, they'll gladly pay a quarter for each one found. So, tell Algie to spend his time searching in high grass. Not only will he make more money for you, he'll be helping the golfers, too. Can't beat that. Better a living shag bag than a dead alligator purse. Have a ball. A whole lot of 'em.

Mama Quail

Dear Mama Quail:

I'm writing to you from the jungles of Brazil, so I hope you get this letter. My harlequin frog is very unhappy. In case you've never seen one, a harlequin frog is bright green with a brilliant yellow chest, ruby red eyes that pop way out and huge feet that look exactly like orange plastic. Everyone laughs at him all the time. He is so sad. He says he wants to run away and hide forever. How can I help him?

Harlick's Mom

Dear Harlick's Mom:

The poor little dear. I checked with the circus people. They said they would love to have Harlick star in their miniature circus. Most children have never seen a harlequin frog, and can you imagine how delighted they would be to see one up close? Harlick could even become the Clown Prince of Frogs. Let me know how it works out. I've seen pictures of harlequin frogs. They are delightful. I hope he enjoys being a clown in a miniature circus. Just think, he doesn't even have to wear a costume. Lots of luck.

Mama Quail

Dear Mama Quail:

My pigeon, Columbia, has to walk to school every day. But he is so pigeon-toed that by the time he gets there, he's late. Don't tell me to get him corrective shoes. They don't help pigeons.

Tired of Writing Excuses

Dear Tired of Writing Excuses:

Where have you been already? Get corrective *skates*. Sure, they'll criss-cross, but at least he'll be rolling. That's faster than walking. Try it. By the way, Columbia sounds like a real little gem.

Mama Quail

Dear Mama Quail:

My name is Fido. I live with people who run a fancy French restaurant. I used to be very happy, but not any more. My masters have decided that Fido is too ordinary a name, so they changed it to Phydeaux. Looks fancy on the menu, but still pronounced Fido. I say menu because at the bottom is a note that says: "Let Phydeaux bring you your doggie bag." Now, when a customer asks for a doggie bag, I have to trot it out to him. As if that's not bad enough, they make me wear a fancy collar with lace and jewelry on it. I could just roll over and die. Of course the customers think it's terrific. They keep telling my owners how cute I am. Mama Quail, I don't want to do this the rest of my life. What should I do? Please don't tell me to run away from home because I'd hate to give up all those good bones.

Just Plain Old Fido

Dear Plain Old Fido:

When you reach the table holding the doggie bag in your jaws, don't let go. Instead, get FRISKY, FRISKY, FRISKY. Dart this way and that way. Wag your tail. *Keep wagging*. And keep ducking each time the customer reaches for the bag. Do this until the restaurant is in an uproar. The customers will be delighted, but your owners will not. Soon, they'll have to give up PHYDEAUX and welcome back plain, old FIDO. Every dog has his day. You'll get yours.

Mama Quail

Dear Mama Quail:

  I'm a zebra, and I live here in the zoo. I'm very contented, except for one thing. Every day, when the camel strolls by, he spits on me. Right in my face! He's on the other side of the fence so I can't kick him. What shall I do?

Stripes But Not Yellow

Dear Stripes But Not Yellow:

  How about hoofing up a nice pile of dirt. When the camel stops to spit, you get ready. Swing around and kick up the pile of dirt right into *his* face. Some of it is bound to land in his open mouth. Keep this up until the camel decides he's had enough biting your dust. Let me know how you make out.

Mama Quail

Dear Mama Quail:

My baby, Chick Pea, collects jelly beans. She puts them in her little nest and sits on them, pretending to hatch eggs. This is fine until the jelly beans melt in the hot hen house. Then, it is all I can do to pull Chick Pea out of that sticky mess. She screams the whole time. Yet no matter what I say, she does the same thing over again. Once she found liquor-flavored jelly beans. When they melted, the fumes mixed with the heat. It made the hens woozy, and they toppled off their nests. It was awful. Help.

Tired of Jelly Bean Meltdown

Dear Tired of Jelly Bean Meltdown:

Baby Chick Pea sounds adorable. Go find some tiny round pebbles and paint them different colors. Or buy some plastic jelly beans from the variety store. Put those into her tiny nest. This will make her feel very happy, and you won't have any more mess. Baby Chick Pea only wants to be "hatching eggs" like her mommie.

Mama Quail

Dear Mama Quail:

My youngest snail is NOT SLOW. All the others are slow as molasses. But not the youngest. In fact, everyone calls him "The Silver Streak." I'm slow too, and there is no way I can keep up with him. He is driving all of us crazy, whizzing around so fast you can hardly see him. What can I do to slow him down? I'd like to have things more normal around here.

Mother Snail

Dear Mother Snail:

I'm really at a loss for words. What I am about to say may upset you. But I can't come up with anything else. ARE YOU SURE HE'S A *SNAIL?*

Mama Quail

P.S.   In the meantime, I will check with my readers. Maybe one of them can recognize what you have. If so, will let you know.

Dear Mama Quail:

You want to see something *pitiful?* Pitiful! A giraffe with whiplash. Now, that's pitiful. My poor baby has to wear a whiplash collar on his entire neck. If that isn't a mess! He dunked a basketball and kept on going. His head and neck followed the ball all the way down to the floor. Was it ever a chore getting him out of that hoop. And that whiplash collar is so hot. How can I make him more comfortable?

Too-Tall Story

Dear Too-Tall Story:

Get a vacuum cleaner with an extra long hose and an extra skinny nozzle. Turn it on plain air and push the nozzle far as you can down into the collar. The nice cool air will give him some relief, and maybe help you keep your cool too.

Mama Quail

P.S.   Can you spare a picture?

Dear Mama Quail:

I knitted some leg warmers for my boyfriend, the ostrich, for his birthday. He refuses to wear them. Says they keep falling down around his ankles and hamper his running. And worst of all, if his friends ever caught him in leg warmers, they'd call him sissy and bury their heads in the sand so they wouldn't have to look at him. I am furious. And I'm not speaking to him until he wears them. Am I wrong?

Pam in Cameroon

Dear Pam in Cameroon:

Welllllll...you probably offended his ostrich ego. He has a point. Why don't you take one of the leg warmers, knit fringes on the ends and give it to him as a nice scarf. As for the other, cut it up into sections and give them to your girl friends to use as *egg* warmers. Save one, for yourself of course, for when you have to leave the nest.

Mama Quail

P.S.   I must admit I would like to have seen a picture of your boyfriend, the ostrich, with leg warmers on.

Dear Mama Quail:

My son, Herman the Termite, plays catcher on his Little League team. Fans call him "Herm the Term." He's a homerun hitter (always hits the ball with the fat of the bat). Coach says he's the most valuable player, and without him there's no chance of the team making it to the Small, Small World Series. But, Mama, Herman has one big fault. Soon as the inning's over, he flips off his mask, grabs the nearest bat and begins chewing. He's nuts about bats. The umpire keeps throwing him out of the game. When that happens, the team always loses. The coach solved the problem by tying Herman's mask on so it can't be taken off until after the game. It sure breaks my heart to see him sitting in the dugout with his mask on. He can't even wipe his nose when it runs. What's a father to do?

Herm the Term's Father

Dear Herm the Term's Father:

The umpire ought to throw the *coach* out of the game. Talk about a "foul" ball. I contacted my baseball expert, Pee Wee Weese, and after he calmed down, Pee Wee said to tell that dumb coach there are aluminum bats and even plastic ones. Some big league teams are using them, too. By the way, the Quail family are real baseball fans, and we'll be rooting for Herm the Term to make it in the Small, Small World Series in WilliamsBug.

Mama Quail

P.S.   You sure struck out with me, Mister. Any guy whose kid plays Little League should have known about aluminum and plastic bats.   MQ

Dear Mama Quail:

Everything is fine in the hen house until nighttime. That's when the fox comes in and tries to steal one of us away for his "pot cluck" dinner. The farmer turns down his hearing aid when he goes to bed, and there's no one else around. No matter how loudly we squawk, he can't hear us. What shall we do? None of us want to wind up as foxy ladies.

> *Marybel*
> *Betty*
> *Pat*
> *Ginny*
> *Phyllis*
> *Joan*
> *Maggie*

Dear Marybel & Company:

You hens will have to out-fox the fox. Hide some eggs from the farmer. Keep them 'til they're rotten. Next time the fox sneaks in, slam him in the face with all the rotten eggs you've got. Eggs with double yolks would be super for this. Show no mercy. He'll give up and won't come near your hen house anymore. Better to lose some eggs than lose some chickens. Incidentally, I checked this out with my chicken man, Prank Ferdoo, and Prankie said it was good advice. Keep scratchin'.

Mama Quail

For those wishing to consult Mama Quail:

Address all questions to:
        Mama Quail
        Creatures Column
        Weekly Territorial
        Southwest, World, 123ABC

If you send a stamped self-addressed envelope, Mama Quail will send you her *Find Your Own Answers* pamphlet. This will be especially useful to those who do not want to reveal their problems in public and those who send in the same question again and again but are never chosen for publication.

Mama Quail does reserve the right to choose among the many letters that come to her and to answer those that seem to be of widest interest.

Please do not ask personal questions about Mama Quail's own life or her family. She will not answer such questions. She absolutely refuses to tell her age or how much money she makes for writing her column.

Index of Mama Quails Correspondents